LOOK OUT FOR THE WHOLE SERIES!

FAMOUS 5
ON THE CASE

THE CASE OF THE
DEFECTIVE DETECTIVE

Hodder
Children's
Books

A division of Hachette Children's Books

**Special thanks to Lucy Courtenay
and Artful Doodlers**

Copyright © 2008 Chorion Rights Limited, a Chorion company

First published in Great Britain in 2008 by Hodder Children's Books

1

A Catalogue record for this book is available from the British Library

ISBN 978 0 340 95981 7

Typeset in Weiss by Avon DataSet Ltd,
Bidford on Avon, Warwickshire

Printed and bound in Great Britain by
Bookmarque Ltd, Croydon, Surrey

The paper and board used in this paperback by Hodder Children's
Books are natural recyclable products made from wood grown in
sustainable forests. The manufacturing processes conform to the
environmental regulations of the country of origin.

Hodder Children's Books
a division of Hachette Children's Books
338 Euston Road, London NW1 3BH
An Hachette Livre UK Company
www.hachettelivre.co.uk

Chapter One

Apart from the fact that everything was upside-down, it was a normal evening in the study at Jo's house.

Timmy the dog was playing with a knotted rope beside the fire as it flickered comfortably in the grate. Jo was building a house of cards, her dark hair falling across her face as she concentrated on balancing the cards just right. Allie was sitting in an armchair, engrossed in a glossy fashion 'n' gossip magazine. And Max was hanging by his feet from the bookcase – hence the upside-down bit – with his digital camera pressed to his face.

"Nope . . ." Max fiddled with the focus, his blond

1

hair hanging down as he zoomed from one cousin to the next. "Nope . . . Nope . . ."

"Max," said Allie in exasperation, laying down her magazine and turning to face the camera, "how do you expect me to learn how movie stars plan to save the environment when you're hanging around like a paparazzi possum?" She paused, brightening. "Oooh!" she said thoughtfully. "That'd be a good cartoon character!"

"It's my photography class assignment," Max explained, still hanging upside-down. *One Hundred Photos – Strange, Interesting or Beautiful.*"

"Ooh," said Allie, immediately keen. "Take *my* picture!"

She rushed over to the hat rack and grabbed a hat and feather boa to use as props, before prancing up and down striking a series of model poses.

Jo glanced up from her card-house and winced. "That definitely counts as 'Strange'," she remarked.

Jo's card-house collapsed as a loud crash sounded from the hall. And the card-house wasn't the only thing to fall down.

"Whooahh – oooph . . ."

Max struggled out of the comfy chair he'd

The last of the cousins, Max, leaped into a sleeping bag and zipped it over his head, so only the top of his tousled blond hair could be seen. Jo grabbed a long metal spoon, stuck a bread roll over each end, then bent the spoon handle to make ear-muffs and slapped them on to her head. Even Timmy the dog covered his ears with his paws.

"OK," Jo said to Allie's back, "full steam ahead."

Allie enthusiastically resumed singing. *"I'll do the cooking, honey,"* she trilled, miming a little stirring at the stove, *"I'll pay the rent . . ."* This part saw her peeling invisible bank notes off a roll. *". . . I know I done you wrong . . ."*

The seagull was back. It poked its head through the door again and listened for a moment. Then it shuddered and flew away with a peeved squawk towards the nearby cliffs that towered along the coastline.

On the top of the cliffs, a dark figure could be seen creeping towards a small building perched perilously close to the cliff edge. The figure peered through the windows, then took out a crowbar and smashed out the glass. An alarm sounded, blaring into the night as he climbed inside.

3

Chapter Two

"I know I'm to blame," Allie belted on into the night. *"Well ain't that a shame, Bill Bailey won't you please come home?"*

The other kids cautiously uncovered their ears as Allie finished. Max poked his head out of his sleeping bag as the coastguard alarm blared in the distance.

"What's that brain-piercing screech?" Max asked, looking fuddled as usual. "Allie's not singing."

"That's the alarm at the coastguard station!" Jo said, scrambling to her feet.

Allie looked offended. "What do you mean 'brain-piercing'?"

"Got to go!" Max shouted, running out of the boat-house with the others in hot pursuit.

They followed the sound up the cliff path to the coastguard station. Then they pushed open the door, found the switch and turned off the alarm. Blissful silence descended on the evening air.

A guard was tied to a chair. He was blindfolded, and appeared to be wearing earplugs.

"Lieutenant Smeade," said Jo in concern, ripping off the blindfold, "are you all right?"

Lieutenant Smeade just stared at the Five. Allie

folded her arms and frowned.

"He's not answering!" she said. "How rude is that? I mean, we're rescuing him and everything."

"He can't hear us," Dylan pointed out. "His ears have been plugged."

Allie didn't look the least bit mollified. "Still," she huffed as Dylan removed the guard's earplugs, "manners are important."

"Don't worry, Lieutenant," Max said, studying the knots which tied the guard's hands to his chair, "I'm an expert at knots. Let's see, this looks like a sheet-bend with a clove hitch and half a sheepshank thrown in. Or is it half a clove hitch with a double reef? Hmmm . . ."

Timmy barked furiously outside the door. The kids turned to look. In the distance, a portly-looking figure was hurrying away, carrying a bag of loot over his shoulder.

"He's got a big belly and a sackful of goodies, but I don't think that's Santa Claus!" said Allie.

Jo, Allie, Dylan and Timmy ran after the thief, leaving Max to struggle on with Lieutenant Smeade's knots.

The stout man huffed and puffed as he pulled the

bag along a dangerous rocky ledge, arriving at a low wooden fence running along the foot of the cliffs. Heaving the bag over the fence, he then struggled to get over it himself, managing to catch his trouser leg on the wooden palings. Unable to free himself, he was forced to leave his trousers behind, revealing white pants gleaming in the moonlight and knee-high black socks.

Jo, Allie, Dylan and Timmy gained a little ground as the figure wriggled out of his trousers. But just as they arrived at the fence, a huge wave crashed on to the rocks – sweeping Allie off her feet.

"Ahhhhh!" Allie squealed as she was pulled out to sea by the rough water.

"Allie!" Jo shouted in horror.

The thief scrambled up the cliff, getting away as Jo, Dylan and Timmy slid down the muddy slope to the rocks. In the water, Allie bobbed up and struggled against the tide.

"It's cold!" Allie gasped as the waves crashed into her. "It's hard to breathe! I'm wearing shrinkable fabrics!"

Jo ripped off her jumper and socks.

"Don't go swimming in there," Dylan advised.

"Allie says the water's terrible."

"I'm making a rope!" Jo explained, tying her socks together. "Give me your clothes!"

Dylan took off his shirt and tied it to the rope. He and Jo threw it out to Allie – but it fell short of her reaching hands.

"Not long enough!" Jo shouted.

"Oh, well . . ." Dylan muttered. Looking embarrassed, he took off his trousers, revealing a pair of teddy-bear-print boxer shorts.

"I'm kinda turning blue out here," Allie chattered over the crashing surf. "And blue skin doesn't go with my accessories."

Timmy seized the free end of the makeshift rope in his teeth and jumped into the water, carrying it to Allie. Jo and Dylan pulled hard, struggling against the violent tide.

"This is a lot of work," Dylan panted, heaving desperately. "Let's just fish for trout next time."

Slowly, they pulled both Allie and Timmy back to shore.

"Thanks," Allie gasped, flopping gratefully on to the rocks. "I'm sorry I fell in the water. That guy got away 'cos of me."

"That's OK," Jo assured her. "We'll get him in the end." Her eyes widened. "Speaking of 'the end'," she added, "you've got a crab on yours."

And Allie leaped to her feet and shrieked as Jo and Dylan tried to pry the large crab off her backside.

Chapter Three

Back in the coastguards' hut, Max was still trying to untie Lieutenant Smeade.

"I think it's 'up, through, around, through, over, through and in'," Lieutenant Smeade said helpfully as Max battled on with the ropes around the coastguard's hands.

Max blew his blond fringe out of his eyes. "Let me try that," he said. "Uh-huh . . .Uh-huh . . . Yup . . ." He paused. "That made the knot bigger!" he complained.

"Still on the knots?" said Jo, as she and the others came back into the hut. "Let me try . . ." She examined the problem, pushing up her sleeves and flexing her fingers. Then she reached over, picked up a pair of scissors from a nearby desk and snipped through the offending ropes.

"Thanks," said Lieutenant Smeade, rubbing his wrists. "What happened to the thief?"

"He ran away," said Allie, looking downcast. "Well, he *waddled* away."

"How could he get away?" Lieutenant Smeade asked in surprise. "He moved slower than a sleeping slug."

"Allie decided to take a little dip," Dylan explained. Water was still dripping from his trousers. "She's very unpredictable."

Allie nodded agreement.

"What did said slow sleepy slug snatch?" Max enquired, looking pleased at the tongue-twist effect.

Lieutenant Smeade looked around the small hut, perplexed. "Huh," he said. "Nothing valuable. A couple of paintings, a few books, a telescope . . ." He jerked upright. "Oh, no!" he gasped. "He grabbed the box file!"

"That sounds serious," said Jo, looking worried.

Lieutenant Smeade slumped despondently back

into his chair. "It is! My sandwich was in it."

"Ooh, what kind of sandwich?" Max asked, his mouth watering slightly. "Turkey? Ham – I bet it was ham!"

Dylan frowned. "So he took some knick-knacks and left equipment like *this*?" He gestured around the room at the blinking electronic equipment. Sliding the computer's CD tray shut, he added: "It's got a multi-core processor and fifteen gigabytes of memory." He looked closer and brightened. "Ooh, and the latest version of *Blasterpod*!"

Dylan settled down and started playing the noisy video game. Looking puzzled, Jo asked the others: "Why would someone go to so much trouble to steal such unimportant stuff?"

"BOOM!" Dylan roared joyfully as Jo, Max and Allie exchanged baffled looks. "In your face, Quadrant Proconsul Zorfan!"

Down on the shore in a secluded, moonlit cove, the thief panted up to a shadowy figure lurking among the rocks.

"I've got the stuff," he wheezed, handing over a CD.

Wordlessly, the figure slid the disk into a laptop computer. Complex technical graphics began scrolling across the screen – ocean maps, complicated charts and diagrams of various coastguard boats.

"Brilliant," said the figure, in an ominous whisper.

"How do we get the information to our ship?" gasped the thief. "They're watching us like hawks."

The figure tapped his fingers thoughtfully on the laptop. "You leave that to me," he murmured. "What's that you've got there?"

"The ham sandwich I stole," said the thief happily, about to tuck in.

"Give it to me," said the figure in the same low whisper. "I'm hungry."

The thief backed away. "No, it's mine . . ."

"No – give it—"

The laptop fell to the ground as they struggled for the sandwich, mysterious coded graphics scrolling soundlessly across its screen.

Chapter Four

The Falcongate theatre was barely recognizable. It had been converted into the set for Tommy Terwilliger's *Talent Tonight* show, and was decked out with game-show glamour: a flashy sign, glittery curtains and coloured spotlights sweeping the stage.

Max, Jo and Timmy were watching from the audience as Constantine Tarlev, owner of the local crazy golf course, performed his terrible juggling act. Wine glasses, tomatoes, eggs and rubber ducks fell in rainbows, bouncing around the stage. Constantine juggled grimly on, clinging to his pride in the face of disaster as only an eternally optimistic Moldovan can.

"Constantine has done many things," Constantine shouted, losing three tomatoes at once. "Never learning to juggle is one of many things Constantine has done."

"So," Max said to Jo, watching Constantine with something between a wince and a grin, "the rules are, each night the worst act gets eliminated?"

Several more objects fell from Constantine's clutching fists.

"Constantine go bye-bye," Max said happily.

"It just doesn't make sense," Jo murmured . . .

"What, that Constantine can't juggle?" Max said, still watching Constantine. "He can't be good at everything – he does make a brilliant doughnut."

Jo shook her head impatiently. "No, Max. The theft." She held up a mobile phone, whose screen glowed in the theatre's darkness. "Look at these pictures Allie took at the crime scene."

She scrolled through the pictures: the computer, a plasma TV, radar and other electronic equipment.

"They left all the valuable electronic stuff," Jo continued as the phone flashed up an image of Max making a monkey-face and posing next to the tied-up and blindfolded Lieutenant Smeade. "There must be *something* we're not thinking of . . ."

While Jo and Max thought this through, Allie waited nervously in the wings. She was studying a sheet of music and rehearsing quietly. Well, as quietly as Allie knew how.

"Do you remember that rainy evening," she warbled. *"I drove you out with nothing but a fine tooth comb—"*

"Did you know the winner of this thing gets a three-hundred brake horsepower Italian sports car?" said Dylan, coming up behind Allie. "VROOOM!"

Allie glanced back at Dylan in surprise. "You can't drive."

"I can when I'm seventeen," Dylan pointed out. "Meanwhile I'll charge kids to sit in it."

On stage, Tommy Terwilliger, game-show host extraordinaire with a tangerine tan and overly white teeth, tipped his straw-boater at the audience and addressed them as Constantine picked up his scattered belongings and slunk off stage.

"Simply super!" Tommy Terwilliger trilled. "Next, a last-minute contestant. The category he picked from 'Tommy's Talent Topper' . . " he tapped his boater hat – " is Romantic Poetry. Here, with a bit of Byron, is Dylan Kyron – er, Kirrin! Simply super!"

Dylan strutted dramatically on stage. A spotlight shone on him as he struck a soulful pose.

"She walks in beauty, like the night/ Of cloudless climes and starry skies . . ." Dylan murmured.

In the audience three girls smiled and sighed, already looking smitten. Dylan upped his romantic approach, playing to the girls.

"And all that's best of dark and bright/ Meet in her aspect and her eyes . . ."

The girls swooned and almost fainted. Max and Jo noticed, and looked at each other in bemusement.

"I know I'm to blame," Allie squawked on behind the curtains. *"Well ain't that a shame; Bill Bailey won't you please come home!"* She revved up for the finish, waving her arms about. *"I'm beggin' ya, Bill! I'm beggin'! Bill Bailey won't you please come boooome!* I got it," she said in triumph, crunching up the song sheet between her fingers, "I've got the song!"

"Allie!" trilled Tommy Terwilliger, hurrying up to her. "I'm changing your song!"

17

Allie looked aghast. "*What?!*"

"This one's *much* better!" said the host. "Wrote it myself! Simply super!"

"OK," Allie said nervously, taking the song and scanning the lyrics. "I'll try." She cleared her throat. "*Swiss wristwatches at the fish-sauce shop . . . ?*" She stopped and frowned at the words. "Oh, man . . ."

As Allie pored over the new song, a very portly technical director hustled up to Tommy Terwilliger. His resemblance to the large, trouserless thief on the cliffs was unmistakable, despite the fact that he was now wearing trousers.

"Mr Terwilliger," Leslie Townes began, "the . . ." He sneezed, coughed, snorted and shook his head. "Allergies acting up," he explained. "This town is full of 'lovely' flowers and 'cute' little animals. I wish they'd cover the whole place with cement."

"Have a cough drop and tell me what's so important," said Tommy Terwilliger.

"The broadcast satellite's on the blink," said Leslie, swigging some red allergy medicine and knocking back a cough drop. "Keeps accidentally showing *The News In Welsh*."

Tommy Terwilliger's orange face hardened. "Not

super!" he growled, sounding remarkably like the shadowy figure in the beach cove. "Not super!"

". . .a heart whose love is innocent," Dylan declaimed, finishing his poem as Tommy Terwilliger and Leslie Townes hurried off together. He bowed gracefully, then threw in an unexpected air-guitar power-chord leap-in-the-air, finishing with the splits.

"Waaaaah!" screamed the three girl fans in the audience.

Dylan swaggered off-stage, passing Allie. "The ladies just love Dylan," he grinned at his cousin. "I'm kind of an impossible act to follow." He clapped Allie on the back. "Well, good luck – you're on."

"Hey," Allie began in alarm. But her cousin was gone.

Chapter Five

Max and Jo stared in horror at the stage.

"Swiss wristwatches at the fish sauce shop don't go together it's true," Allie bellowed, performing her socks off. *"But north and south do, five and ten do, so do me and you . . ."*

Max sank down in his chair as Allie revved up for the big finish.

"SO DO MEEE AND YO-O-O-UUU!" Allie squawked.

In the audience, Timmy was transfixed. So transfixed in fact that he joined in as Allie sang *"YO-O-O-UUU!"* with a matching howl of his own. Allie smiled winningly and bowed to the pained, half-hearted applause rippling through the theatre.

Max leaned over to Jo. "That was really unbelievable, wasn't it?" he said, sounding stunned.

"Yes," Jo said faintly. "I didn't think she could *possibly* get worse."

It was the moment of truth. Tommy Terwilliger led the contestants back on to the stage to join Allie: Dylan; Constantine; local rich-kids Blaine and Daine Dunston, in flashy outfits; Constable Stubblefield, holding a unicycle; and a contortionist who walked on his hands with his legs wrapped around his head.

21

"Simply super!" warbled Tommy Terwilliger. "But sad to say, one of you has to 'get the boot'!"

The audience laughed as Terwilliger put on a big, foam-rubber boot and walked behind the line of performers. "And I'm sorry to tell you, Allie . . ." he trilled as Allie looked apprehensive – ". . .that it's Constantine Tarlev!"

The foam-rubber boot flew out and kicked Constantine in the behind. Constantine slipped and fell on to his backside.

"Ooooph," Constantine mumbled philosophically, "Constantine takes life as it comes."

The others looked relieved and trooped off-stage. Dylan's female fans were waiting for him, holding out objects for him to sign.

"Can we have your autograph?" squealed the first girl. "And a kiss? And your shirt?"

"Easy, ladies," Dylan grinned. "I always have time for my – hey!"

The second girl snipped off a big lock of Dylan's hair as the third girl ripped off his shirt. Clambering over both the others, the first girl kissed Dylan on the cheek, and they all rushed off, giggling breathlessly.

Dylan looked stunned. He felt the side of his head, where his hair was missing. "As long as they don't take anything that doesn't grow back . . ." he muttered.

In George's boat-house that night, the Five were deep in thought. Jo paced back and forth with Timmy at her heels. Dylan was surfing the internet for information on the items that had been stolen from the coastguards' hut. He brought up a nautical-looking website, which played a tinny version of the *Sailor's Hornpipe* in a loop.

"All the stolen stuff was cheap reproductions," Dylan said, pushing back from the computer for a minute. "The paintings were only worth a few pounds, and that's mostly for the frames." He paused, listening as the hornpipe jollied around for the twentieth time. "Catchy tune, though."

He started humming the hornpipe tune.

"I can't resist it," Max confessed, his toes tapping as the hornpipe wound up for a twenty-first rendition.

"I *can* resist it," Jo growled, hitting the "Speaker Off" key on Dylan's keyboard and silencing the maddening little jig.

23

Ignoring the fact that he no longer had any music, Max danced around the room. Dylan returned to the keyboard, typing with a steady *clack-clack* sound.

"Hey," said Jo, suddenly realizing. "That's it! That's why Lieutenant Smeade had earplugs! Computers are noisy when you use them."

"And the thief didn't want Lieutenant Smeade to know he was using the computer," Allie nodded. "I wonder what he was looking at?"

"I bet it's that video of a pig riding a surfboard," Max said, starting to laugh. "That's a crack-up. Aloha-Oink! Aloha-Oink!"

"Whatever it was," Dylan said as Max collapsed into giggles, "he burned it on to a CD. The computer's CD tray was open. "

"So he wanted information, and he didn't want Lieutenant Smeade to know he was getting it," Jo concluded. "And he stole the other stuff as a diversion."

Max fought to regain a serious face. "Brilliant, Jo," he said nodding. The sides of his mouth started twitching again as he turned back to Dylan. "Seriously," he snorted, "find the surfing pig.

24

I can't get enough of it."

Footsteps outside echoed through the still night air. The Five exchanged alert looks. Then they grabbed a large fishing net and hid to one side of the door. As an unseen figure entered, the kids threw the net and caught the intruder.

"Hello, dears," said Jo's mother George brightly from beneath the folds of fishing net. "This basket arrived by special delivery from 'Dylan's Dolls'." She set down the package in front of Dylan.

"Ahh," Jo said, starting to grin as the others rushed to untangle George. "Dylan's fan club sent him a present."

The cousins opened the package eagerly, taking out the goodies: flowers, a mug, a teddy-bear wearing a T-shirt with a heart on it and a jar of what looked like brown goo.

"Some lovely daisies, a jar of sludge . . ." said George, studying the contents of the package. "They claim it's your favourite treat."

"Sludge?" said Dylan in confusion. "I said I liked *fudge*."

"If you don't want it, can I have it?" Max asked eagerly, taking the sludge from Dylan and tucking

25

it away.

"OK, so they went a little overboard about me," Dylan said. "I bet it's out of their system now."

"I'll take that bet . . ." Jo said, staring out of the open door. She pointed down to the beach, where there was an enormous sand-sculpture depicting Dylan in an heroic pose. Battery-operated torches stuck in the sand illuminated the sculpture from beneath.

And standing around the sculpture were Dylan's Dolls themselves, arms crossed, staring hungrily toward the boat-house and their hero.

"There he is!" shrieked one of them. "Dylan! We love you!"

The girls ran screaming towards the boat-house. Looking thoroughly alarmed, Dylan slammed the door shut and pressed his back against it.

"You're a heartthrob now, Dylan," Allie giggled. "Congratulations."

"I've never been more terrified," said Dylan, looking sweaty.

The girls' hands smashed through the door, groping for Dylan. He fled in panic, dived out of an open window and raced away into the night.

26

Chapter Six

Night two of *Talent Tonight* was in full swing. On stage, the Dunston twins were doing an overly dramatic cha-cha in hideous matching costumes that flashed with sequins.

"I wonder what the thief wanted *coastguard* information for," Jo mused, stroking Timmy's head. "Identity theft, maybe?"

Max stared at the stage, where the Dunstons were busy stumbling and knocking over the set dressing. "What *I* wonder is, who's going to get the boot tonight?" he said.

Jo pulled herself back to the talent contest with an effort. "It's got to be those Dunstons," she said.

"Unless they win first prize for 'Most Creepy'."

Backstage, Allie was warming up her voice. "La-la-la," she sang, sounding like a winded bullfrog as usual. "La-la-la-laaaaaaa . . ."

"Allie!" Tommy Terwilliger hurried up to her, clutching another sheet of music. "I've written another new song for you! I get chills, it's so simply super!"

Allie took the sheet and read the words. "Ha!" she said. "He rhymed 'ukulele' and 'Ben Disraeli'. That's great!" She paused, frowning. "Who's 'Ben Disraeli'?"

"And now, ladies and gentlemen," said Tommy Terwilliger up on the stage, "the simply super song-stylings of . . . Allie!"

There was a smattering of weak applause as Allie walked on-stage.

"Her again?!" mumbled a member of the audience. "Me 'ead still hurts!"

Jo prepared herself by covering her ears with her hands. Timmy buried his head under a seat cushion. Looking smug, Max reached under his seat, produced a deerstalker cap, put it on and tied the flaps down over his ears.

"Where'd you get that?" Jo demanded.

28

"Sorry," said Max cheerfully, "can't hear you."

"Give me that!" Jo begged, trying to wrestle the hat off Max's head.

"Hi, everybody," Allie smiled up on stage. "Tonight, I'm going to sing . . ." She studied her new song sheet. ". . .*When In Rome!*"

Out in the ocean, a large trawler was ploughing through the waves. In the trawler's dark control station, two shifty-looking individuals watched the broadcast on a small TV.

"*When In Rome*," one of them said. "That means the message tonight'll be a Caesar Shift code."

The other – a man – prepared to take notes as Allie launched into her song.

"*In Hawaii I like strumming on a ukulele,*" she belted with gusto, "*In London, love the statue of old Ben Disraeli, love to drive my fancy car really fast at home, but I only want to dance with you when I'm in Rome!*"

The two smugglers quickly entered information into a computer, bringing up a set of complex nautical graphics.

"The coastguard anti-smuggling ship is patrolling ten miles north-west of us," grinned the man.

The first smuggler nodded. "So we land the sports cars at fifty, nineteen, fifty-two north; four, thirty-five, three west." She paused and frowned at the small screen. "This really is criminal."

The second smuggler looked surprised at his companion's sudden stab of conscience. "That's why we get paid a lot," he pointed out.

The first smuggler shook her head. "Not the smuggling," she said. "The way that girl sings. Ugh."

Back in the theatre, it was Constable Stubblefield's turn to shine in the talent contest. She was riding around the stage on a unicycle and hula-hooping at the same time. It was impressive.

Backstage, Dylan watched Constable Stubblefield's performance in amusement. A stagehand wheeled a giant cake up to him.

"For *moi*?" Dylan said in surprise. He smiled and reached out to try the icing, but someone suddenly popped out of the cake. Well, three someones.

"We love you, Dylan!" screamed Dylan's Dolls. "You belong to us forever!"

"I'm not Dylan," Dylan choked out as his three fans grabbed him and smothered him in kisses. "I, uh, just look like him!"

He scrambled up the side of the cake and jumped inside. The wheeled platform on which the cake sat promptly rolled off up a corridor, chased by the girls. Halfway along, Dylan leaped out, grabbing a pipe which ran along the ceiling. He hung quietly from it as his screaming fans raced by beneath him. Dylan waited until they had disappeared, then swung off the pipe.

"Woaahhhh!" Dylan shrieked, kicking open a door and landing in one of the theatre offices.

Not taking any chances, he slammed the door

behind him and tried to catch his breath as he flopped down on to the sofa.

"OW!" he roared, leaping straight up again. He picked up the object he'd sat on – a broken piece of mast off a model ship. As he was about to toss the piece of mast away, he stopped. A broken ship model lay in the bin. Dylan's eyes widened. He had seen it before, when he'd been visiting the coastguard!

Without wasting another second, Dylan started to search the office. Behind the sofa, he found a large bag.

"This is the stuff from the coastguard station!" Dylan exclaimed, staring at the cheap reproduction paintings and the little spyglass that Lieutenant Smeade had described to the Five.

The door banged open, startling Dylan.

"What are you doing in my office?" demanded Leslie Townes, snuffling and sneezing into a voluminous handkerchief.

Dylan held up the bag of loot. "Discovering you're a thief," he said.

Chapter Seven

Leslie Townes frowned angrily and swiped the bag away, moving nimbly for a large man. Dylan gave chase.

Backstage, Allie was helping herself to a snack from the food table. She saw Leslie charging towards her and jumped out of his way just in time. Stopping briefly to grab a doughnut, Leslie hurried along. As Dylan raced past in pursuit, Allie abandoned her snack and joined in the chase.

Leslie plunged on to the stage, barging into Constable Stubblefield who was still riding around on her unicycle. As Allie and Dylan leaped through the curtains, Leslie pushed the police officer off her unicycle, causing her to get tangled up in her hula hoop.

"Whooaahh!" squealed Constable Stubblefield. Leslie Townes had mounted the unicycle and was wobbling off at speed. "Hey! That's my grandmother's unicycle!"

The audience clapped and laughed. Timmy barked urgently. Max and Jo stopped grinning and looked alert.

"Max, I don't think that was part of the show," Jo said, grabbing her cousin's hand. "Come on!"

And they raced out of a side exit with Timmy close behind.

On the outskirts of Falcongate, Leslie Townes was still hanging on to his bag of loot while balancing on the unicycle. Huffing and puffing, he wove and wobbled about, riding in circles as he tried to keep his balance. The Five ran after him as he pedalled down the road.

An artist had set up his easel on the pavement several hundred metres from the theatre and was attempting to capture Falcongate's main street by night. The out-of-control unicyclist crashed straight through the painting, sending easel, brushes, paints and hapless artist flying. The Five put on a burst of speed. They were catching up. Seeing that he was losing ground, Leslie tried to trick his pursuers by turning off the main street – but found he was heading straight down a steep set of steps.

"Ow ow ow ow ow ow," Leslie wailed, his cheeks wobbling as he bounced down each step. The bag was shaken from his grasp, and its contents spilled everywhere. Still in hot pursuit, the Kirrins caught each item as it rained down on them.

"There's no ham sandwich here," said Max in disappointment. "What a rip-off."

At the bottom of the steps, Leslie fell off the unicycle, but got up just as a big lorry rumbled down the road towards him. He managed to heave himself up on to the lorry's bumper and waved victoriously as the lorry roared away.

"So long, losers!" he crowed, leaping inside the lorry.

There was a violent snapping sound. Dozens of crustaceous claws reached up into view, clicking fiercely. Leslie had managed to hitch a ride with a hundred live and extremely angry crabs and lobsters.

"YEEEOOOOOOOOOWWWWWW!" Leslie howled, leaping into the air covered in nipping shellfish. "Ouch-ouch-ouch!"

The Five watched, gratified. They might not have caught Leslie Townes, but there was something to be said for watching him leaping around in pain.

"Well," Jo said with a grin, "at least he got pinched."

Backstage in the theatre, Constable Stubblefield was still trying to extricate herself from her hula-hoop. Tommy Terwilliger looked on, his face turning a paler shade of orange as the kids set out all the recovered loot on a table.

"I can't believe Leslie Townes is a thief," Tommy Terwilliger declared, looking twitchy as he said it. "*Un*-super! If I see hide or hair of him, I'll tell the Constable immediately."

"Rolling away!" shouted Constable Stubblefield, as the hula-hoop got the better of her and took off with her still inside. "Someone help me arrest this thing!"

Chapter Eight

Right outside the theatre door the following day, Dylan's Dolls circled like sharks on the pavement, scanning the streets hungrily for their hero.

"Hi girls," Jo said, as she and Allie rolled a huge marching-band bass drum past the Dolls and towards the stage door. "Isn't that Dylan a dreamboat?" She clawed the air, adding: "*Rrrrrooww.*"

The Dolls sighed and swooned, and Allie and Jo pushed the drum inside the theatre. Max was already there, happily snacking at the food table while Timmy wolfed down a hamburger behind him. Allie bent down to the drum.

"You're safe, little drummer boy," she said

through the drum's membrane.

There was a tearing sound. Dylan broke out of the drum and sighed with relief. "I've said it before and I'll say it again," he said, brushing himself down. "Girls are just plain dangerous."

Jo thwacked him warningly with the drumstick.

"Owww," said Dylan. He turned to Max. "See what I mean?"

"Mmmmmph-mheee-hrmmmmuh-hmmmp," Max nodded, his mouth still full of food.

"My point exactly," Dylan said, sounding injured. He brightened as he spotted something on the table. "Oooh," he said and licked his lips, "liquorice!"

Making towards the food table, Dylan promptly slipped in a puddle of gooey red liquid and landed on his backside. "Yuk!" he complained.

"Smells like medicine," said Max, lifting Dylan back on to his feet.

Allie and Jo stepped up to look at the mess, noticing various medications and wrappers lying on the floor.

"Sneeze-B-Quiet . . ." Jo read a couple of labels. "Allerg-Easy."

"These are allergy medicines," Allie said, twirling a label between her fingers. "Leslie Townes was complaining about his allergies!"

Down in the bowels of the theatre, they heard an echoey, booming sound.

"*Wha-choo! . . .Fwha-shoo! . . .Bah-fmwhew! . . Fmeh! . . .Gnuh! . . .*"

Following the sound of explosive sneezing, the Five tiptoed down the hall and peered around the corner. They saw Leslie Townes leaving his office. Between sneezes, he was laughing and joking with . . .

"Tommy Terwilliger!" Dylan gasped as they recognized the tangerine-coloured TV host. "They're in this together!"

Leslie and Terwilliger shook hands. As they went out together, the Five exchanged shocked looks. What was going on?

"Allie," Jo said as soon as Leslie and Terwilliger were out of sight, "you and Timmy stay here and keep a lookout. We'll see what we can find in Terwilliger's office."

"Simply super!" Allie said, mocking Tommy Terwilliger.

Jo, Max and Dylan pushed open the door to Terwilliger's office. It was pretty spartan. There was a small table with a computer on it, a chair, and on a hatstand hung an overcoat and a raincoat.

"Not much here to search through," said Max. He poked around, looked at the table, moved the chair a fraction and peered underneath it. "Done," he said, straightening up. "Whew, I'm done in."

Dylan cracked his knuckles. "Allow me," he said, sitting down.

As Dylan began to type away at Tommy Terwilliger's computer inside the office, Timmy growled outside the door. Allie broke off from humming her "Fish Sauce" tune and looked along the corridor.

"Allie!" Tommy Terwilliger gushed. "Super to see you!" He added more brusquely: "What are you doing down here?"

"Um . . .vocal exercises?" said Allie, panicking. "Good acoustics in the basement. I sing people's names. Like . . .*Ma-ry Smith* . . .*Per-cy Pike* . . .And of course – *TERWILLIGER!*" She stood a little closer to the closed door to Terwilliger's office.

"TERWILLIGER! TERRRR-WILLIGER!" she bellowed as loudly as she could.

Inside the office, Dylan, Jo and Max traded looks. Uh-oh . . .

"Super . . ." said Terwilliger, looking mystified. Pushing past Allie, he entered his office and glanced around. The Kirrins were nowhere to be seen. He looked a little more relaxed, and headed to his computer. As he tapped some keys, concentrating on the monitor, the hat stand scooted across the floor and out of the door.

"Dylan," said Jo, extricating herself from the hat stand, "did you find anything on the computer?

"Didn't have time," Dylan said. He held up a memory stick. "So I downloaded the whole thing."

In the boat-house that evening, everyone crowded round Dylan as he transferred information from his memory stick on to his laptop. He clicked on a folder, bringing up several windows with pages upon pages of information: ID charts of coastguard ships, maps of the coast and tide-tables.

"The coastguard data," Max cheered. "Ha – you stole the stolen information!"

Dylan shrugged. "I'm a show-business star. We behave abominably."

Clicking on another folder, he opened a different window. This one listed tables of letters.

"A equals K, B equals L . . ." Allie read.

"These are cipher keys, for secret codes," Jo said in excitement. She turned to Allie. "And look – that file has your song lyrics."

Dylan typed something else, then studied the screen. "Allie's been singing in code," he said. "Look what the song says if you plug in the A-to-K cipher."

"Anti-smuggling ships . . . north-west . . . Deliver Italian cars . . ." Max translated slowly.

"They're using Allie to pass information to smugglers!" Jo gasped.

Allie frowned. "But why would Tommy Terwilliger work with smugglers? Doesn't he have enough money?"

"With these people there's no such thing as enough," Dylan informed his cousin. "Personal submarines, a house made of chocolate . . ."

The others goggled at him. Dylan looked defensive. "That's how *I'm* going to blow my money when *I* make it big," he said.

"So that's why I haven't 'got the boot'," Allie said. "They've been using me." She looked downcast. "I'm not a good singer at all, am I?"

Dylan, Max and Jo all started up as kindly as they could. "Hey, listen . . ." "You're not that . . ." "You have a very . . ."

"Well actually, no," Jo said at last. "But you're a good person and ooh, you really know how to use make-up."

Allie sighed. "I don't care if I'm good or not," she said resolutely. "I think I should sing one more song on the show." Her eyes started twinkling as the others looked intrigued. "Something *we* write . . ."

Chapter Nine

Back on *Talent Tonight* that evening, Allie stepped up on to the stage.

"Hello, Falcongate!" she said cheerfully. "Hit it, Maestro."

Music started playing. Allie crumpled up the song sheet Tommy Terwilliger had given her, and starting belting out: *"I saw you on my big screen plasma TV, my love for you ain't analog it's strictly HD . . ."*

Tommy Terwilliger frowned in the wings. "That's not the song I gave her!" he muttered. As he marched towards the stage, Timmy blocked him and growled ferociously. Terwilliger froze.

"Sorry about the last-minute lyric change,

Tommy," said Jo, as she and Max stepped up to the show host. "We wanted to communicate a very special message."

"*I busted my remote so I can never turn you off,*" Allie roared on joyfully.

Out at sea, the trawler rolled and dipped. The smugglers were watching their TV as usual, taking notes and entering information into the computer.

"We drop the goods at Cormorant Point," said the first smuggler, pointing to the map that was

pinned up in their control room. "That's just a few minutes away."

The trawler altered its course, turning towards the shore and accelerating through the waves. Within minutes, it had eased up to a remote dock, and cut the engines.

"Hiya, lads," called the first smuggler out to the shore, holding a line on the deck. "We've got some lovely plasma screen tellies tonight."

She tossed the line towards the dock.

"Isn't that nice?" said Constable Stubblefield, catching the line deftly. "I'll count that as part of your confession. Hands up, please."

Police officers swarmed over the deck of the trawler as the second smuggler joined his colleague on the deck and they both raised their hands. Constable Stubblefield pulled out her mobile.

"Hello, young Kirrin," she said cheerfully into the receiver. "They were right where your song sent them."

"Thanks, Constable Stubblefield," Jo grinned, still backstage at the theatre. She snapped her phone shut and gave an "OK" sign to Allie, who was still out on stage in front of the glittery curtain.

"... *Our love is brighter and sharper, and the images never*—" Seeing Jo's sign, Allie abruptly stopped singing. "Thank you, good night!" she called out into the auditorium. "Tommy Terwilliger's a big old crook. And now, the Dancing Dunstons!"

As Allie hurried off-stage, the curtain behind her rose to reveal the Dunstons, prepared for a King Kong-themed ballroom dance. Daine was dressed as a platinum blonde, Blaine as a gorilla in a big cage, all in front of a cardboard mock-up of the top of the Empire State Building. As the foxtrot music started up and Blaine "escaped" from the cage and started dancing with his sister, Tommy Terwilliger ran across the stage with Jo and Max close behind him. Terwilliger collided with the Dunstons, who spun away from each other in confusion.

"Hey!" Jo struggled to get away from a dazed Blaine, who had grabbed her by mistake to continue the dance.

Daine meanwhile seized Max.

"Oh, hello . . ." said Max, finding himself twirled across the stage. The Empire State Building wobbled alarmingly.

Terwilliger had made it across the stage, and was

now heading for an exit. But Allie, Dylan and Timmy stepped out from behind the wings, blocking his way. He twisted into a detour, shinned up a curtain rope and headed for the catwalks overhead.

Now it was Dylan's turn to run on to the stage. On cue, Dylan's Dolls screamed and swooned. Ignoring them, Dylan clambered up the cardboard Empire State Building, then leaped up to get a handhold on the overhead catwalk. As Dylan hooked his leg over the lighting rig, Max and Jo at last managed to disengage themselves from the dancing Dunstons. Ploughing on, the Dunstons found each other again and doggedly continued their number.

Terwilliger swung himself on to the catwalk above the place where Dylan now stood. Dylan chased after him as best he could, crawling across the catwalk. Terwilliger spun around and shone a spotlight in Dylan's face.

"Owww," Dylan yelled, covering his blinded eyes in pain. "I thought I'd love the spotlight. Instead, it's burning the eyes out of my skull!"

Below, Allie and Jo grabbed on to a curtain rope.

Max heaved on the pulley to hoist them up.

"Going up!" Max shouted, starting to hoist his cousins into the air.

Allie and Jo rode the rope gracefully up to the catwalk.

"I think this is our floor . . ." Jo announced.

Terwilliger turned to see them as they joined Dylan on the catwalk. He grabbed a huge sandbag suspended from a rope and swung it at them, forcing them to climb quickly down a couple of ladders to get out of the way. The sandbag swung back and clobbered Dylan instead. He was knocked off the catwalk, but managed to grab on to it as he fell.

"Owww," Dylan yelled, swinging twenty feet above the stage. "Ehhhh . . ."

Tommy Terwilliger stood directly above Dylan. His face glowed even more demonically than usual. "You're about to be a very 'big hit' on-stage," he tittered, and prepared to tread on Dylan's hand.

Chapter Ten

"Leave Dylan alone!" screamed one of Dylan's Dolls.

Somehow, Dylan's fans had made it on to the catwalk. They swarmed on to Tommy Terwilliger in a wave of hairspray and perfume.

"Aaggghh!" Terwilliger screeched. "Get off me!"

"Wow," said Dylan, still swinging above the stage and watching in admiration as Terwilliger struggled to fight off the girls. "I'd heard how piranhas can strip a cow down to its skeleton in thirty seconds, but I could never really picture it before."

Terwilliger managed at last to wriggle away from the enraged Dolls. As he staggered off along the catwalk, the Dolls helped pull Dylan up on to the catwalk.

"Thanks, girls," Dylan said gratefully. "I owe you one."

Limping slightly now, Terwilliger arrived at a ladder leading to a lower catwalk. As he climbed down, Allie scurried up from below, placing a rope-noose on one of the lower rungs. As soon as the game-show host's foot stepped into the noose . . .

"Now!" Allie yelled.

Further along the catwalk, Jo yanked the rope, which ran over a pulley. Terwilliger's feet were pulled out from under him, and he swung, upside down, behind the Dunstons' dance act.

"Woahhhhh," Tommy Terwilliger wailed, missing the Empire State Building by inches.

"You know what they say about show-biz," said Jo in satisfaction. "You have to learn the ropes."

Leslie Townes was backstage, still unaware of the ruckus, approaching the food table while putting eye drops in his puffy red eyes. In disbelief, he spotted Terwilliger out on-stage, dangling by his ankle.

"Oh boy . . ." said Leslie in alarm, and hustled

towards an exit.

Timmy blocked his way with a menacing growl.

"Going somewhere, Mister?" Max asked, coming alongside Timmy.

"Er, yes," said Leslie, eyeing Timmy nervously. "I was heading – that way."

He pointed away from Timmy, towards the stage.

"You'd better hurry," Max advised, making a big show of holding tightly on to Timmy. "I can barely hold him."

Leslie backed out on-stage, followed by Max pretending to struggle with the growling Timmy – straight into the open gorilla cage. As soon as he was inside, Jo, Dylan and Allie swung down on ropes from overhead and kicked the cage door shut.

"Hey," Tommy Terwilliger whined, still hanging upside-down beside the cage. "What about me?"

Jo produced the big, foam-rubber boot. "Looks like it's your turn to get the boot," she said, putting it on and booting him in the behind so that the game-show host swung towards the cage.

"Owwww," Tommy Terwilliger wailed.

Dylan opened the door. Terwilliger swung into the cage, where the rope came off his foot and dropped him on top of his portly accomplice.

"Oooffff!" Tommy grunted.

"Ooooof!" Leslie Townes agreed. "You need to lose some weight."

Dylan shut the door on the pair. "Ta-da!"

On cue, the Dunstons' dance music ended. The audience, believing the entire spectacle had been part of the show, applauded mightily. The Kirrins and the Dunstons, in a tableau in front of the caged bad guys, acknowledged the applause and all took a graceful bow.

Dylan glanced to the wings. The Dolls were screaming and blowing kisses.

"They saved me up there," Dylan said to Jo as he beckoned the girls to join them on stage. "The least I can do is give them a little hug."

He opened his arms to the squealing girls. But they rushed straight past him.

"Max!" screamed the first girl. "You're so good with animals! You're so sensitive! We love you!"

Max was still holding Timmy's collar. He looked at Timmy as the girls swarmed towards them. "Let's get out of here!" he said hurriedly, and fled with Timmy close beside him as the Dolls chased them around the stage.

"Hey Max!" wailed the girls. "Come back Max! We love you Max!"

"Hi, Mum!" Jo shouted, happily waving as Max and Timmy tore past with the Dolls still hot on their heels.

Back at home, George watched fondly as the cousins bowed to the whooping audience and waved at the camera. "I have to say," she said, "that's what I call good, old-fashioned entertainment."

Epilogue

Jo focused the videocamera. "Sticky Situation Number Twenty-Nine," she announced. "You Have To Send A Coded Message."

Allie and Max stood outside George's house in front of the camera.

"There are lots of ways to send coded messages, even if you don't have a phone or a computer," Allie began.

"For instance," Max continued, "there's semaphore."

Jo panned to where Dylan was waving a couple of flags way off in the distance.

Max started translating.

"England . . . expects . . ."

Dylan waved the flags faster.

"Rumpelstiltskin," Max tried, looking perplexed. "Cabbage lips pea-pie-po."

Jo zoomed the lens closer to Dylan, who was now looking frantic. "I think the message is – he's being chased by a wasp," she informed the others.

Dylan was indeed waving the flags to shoo away a wasp. As the others turned to watch, he gave up and fled, running straight into a tree with a thump.

THE CASE OF THE
MEDIEVAL MEATHEAD

Read on for
Chapter One of the
Famous 5's next
Case File . . .

Hodder Children's Books

A division of Hachette Children's Books

Chapter One

The morning sun flooded the beautiful tree-covered island. Wispy white clouds scudded through the perfectly blue sky. On a hill above the harbour, a magnificent castle spread its crenellated shadow across a collection of brightly coloured, medieval-style tents. Pennants fluttered in the breeze.

"Avalon Island," Jo declared. "An idyllic weekend for the whole family."

"And a wicked trip back in time to the thrill-filled Middle Ages!" Max said approvingly.

Inside one of the colourful tents, a young man wearing a crown and doublet and holding a sceptre was waving regally to assembled onlookers. A

THE CASE OF ALLIE'S
REALLY VERY BAD SINGING

Hodder
Children's
Books

A division of Hachette Children's Books

Special thanks to Lucy Courtenay
and Artful Doodlers

A Catalogue record for this book is available from the British Library

ISBN 978 0 340 95981 7

Typeset in Weiss by Avon DataSet Ltd,
Bidford on Avon, Warwickshire

Printed and bound in Great Britain by
Bookmarque Ltd, Croydon, Surrey

The paper and board used in this paperback by Hodder Children's
Books are natural recyclable products made from wood grown in
sustainable forests. The manufacturing processes conform to the
environmental regulations of the country of origin.

Hodder Children's Books
a division of Hachette Children's Books
338 Euston Road, London NW1 3BH
An Hachette Livre UK Company
www.hachettelivre.co.uk

LOOK OUT FOR THE WHOLE SERIES!

Case Files 11 & 12: The Case of the Medieval Meathead & The Case of the Messy Mucked Up Masterpiece

Case Files 13 & 14: The Case of the Guy Who Makes You Act Like a Chicken & The Case of the Felon with Frosty Fingers

Case Files 15 & 16: The Case of the Bogus Banknotes & The Case of Eight Arms and No Fingerprints

Case Files 17 & 18: The Case of the Flowers That Make Your Body All Wobbly & The Case of the Guy Who Looks Pretty Good for a 2000 Year-Old

Case Files 19 & 20: The Case of the Gobbling Goop & The Case of the Surfer Dude Who's Truly Rude

Case Files 21 & 22: The Case of the Cactus, the Coot, and the Cowboy Boot & The Case of the Seal Who Gets All Up In Your Face

Case Files 23 & 24: The Case of the Snow, the Glow, and the Oh, No! & The Case of the Fish That Flew the Coop

Chapter One

It was a warm night, and the Kirrin cousins were camping in Jo's boat-house down by the beach. The doors were flung wide open to show the moonlit sea, and an assortment of camping gear littered the ground: sleeping bags, lanterns and a large supply of snacks.

Allie tossed her long blond hair over her shoulders and cleared her throat. *"Won't you come home, Bill Bailey?"* she sang tunelessly, attempting a well-known old American song. *"Won't you come home? I cried the whole day long . . ."*

A seagull flew into the boat-house. It landed on the ground, folded away its large white wings and

1

studied Allie with interest. Briefly thrown, Allie stopped singing and stared at the bird. It stared unblinkingly back.

"I think it has your singing confused with a lady-seagull's mating cry," said Allie's cousin Jo.

"Sorry, Mr Seagull," said Allie, shooing the bird away, "I don't have time for dating right now. I have to practise for Tommy Terwilliger's *Talent Tonight* show."

Jo sat up and pushed a hand through her dark brown hair. "What, that TV thing?" she said in disbelief.

"Yeah," Allie said happily. "It's coming to Falcongate. I'm singing on it tomorrow night."

"Tomorrow?" Dylan said, pushing his glasses up his nose. "You need a *lot* more practice."

Ignoring him – after all, Dylan was the nerdiest of her cousins – Allie opened her mouth to sing again.

"Wait!" Dylan said, scrambling up as Allie took a deep breath. "Face the sea – it's like singing in the shower, but there's a lot more water."

Allie shrugged and turned to face out of the door. When he was sure Allie couldn't see him, Dylan grabbed a pillow and folded it over his ears.

2

landed in as Jo, Allie and Timmy all rushed from the study into the hall. Dylan was sitting at the foot of the stairs, rubbing his head, surrounded by a dozen books. His glasses sat crooked on his nose.

"Ooh," he said groggily.

"Dylan!" Jo said in concern. "Are you all right?"

"Couldn't see over the pile of books," Dylan mumbled, still rubbing his head. "Now I have a bump."

"Close-up of a bump!" Max said, struck with inspiration as the others moved to help Dylan up. "It'll look like Mount Everest!" And he snapped a shot of Dylan's head.

"Ooooh," Dylan moaned, blinking at the ferocity of the flash. "Now I have a bump *and* I'm blind."

"*The Case Of The Missing Millionaire: An Abelard B. Covington Mystery*," Jo read, picking up one of the scattered books and reading the jacket.

"He's only seventeen, but he's the world's greatest detective!" Dylan said. His voice oozed with admiration.

"I've heard of him," Max said. "He solves impossible cases, then he turns them into bestsellers!"

3

"He's signing his latest bestseller in town tomorrow," Dylan said eagerly. "I bet he's even richer than old man Dunston . . ."

A short distance away, an imposing manor house stood in the evening chill, its gravel drive raked to perfection and a line of woodland to one side. Standing in the slanting moonlit shadows of the woodland, a dark figure observed the house, whose windows glowed with rich light.

"Dunston Manor," said the figure thoughtfully to himself. "Time to make High-and-Mighty Mister Dunston a little less wealthy . . ." And he reached into a kit-bag and produced a crowbar, before padding silently across the wide, soft lawn.

Chapter Two

In the centre of Falcongate the next day, a queue of people stretched through the door of the bookshop and along the street. A plump lady constable was observing the crowd with a ferocious eye and a large truncheon in her hand.

"All right, you lot," Constable Stubblefield barked, "stay orderly, or I'll be forced to make free with my truncheon. *Niii-haa!*"

She waved her baton ninja-style, to impress people with her truncheon skills. Satisfied that she'd made her point to the wide-eyed crowd, she then leaned against a lamp-post, produced a paperback book with its cover folded back, and started to read, swinging her baton menacingly all the while.

Falcongate rarely saw this kind of interest in a bookshop event. As a result, the local news crew was on the scene.

"Falcongate is buzzing about the imminent arrival of the famous Abelard," said local reporter Polly Lucas breathlessly to camera. Her chimpanzee sidekick Prince Extremely Hairy yawned and scratched himself. "Even our own Constable Stubblefield is a fan," Polly continued, pointing at the police officer.

Constable Stubblefield looked up from her book. "Pshaw," she said, offended. "Why would I read a crime book? Give me a quicksilver, daffodil-scented romance any day."

Bored with scratching, Prince Extremely Hairy leaped up and snatched the novel from Constable Stubblefield's grasp. He made off with it clutched in his hairy paws.

"Hey, you flea-bitten rat with thumbs!"Constable Stubblefield yelled, giving chase. "The Geisha Princess is about to marry a pirate!"

Inside the bookshop, the cousins and Timmy were at the head of the queue. A desk piled with copies of

Abelard's new book had been set up for the signing.

"I've been standing here so long, my legs are asleep," Max complained. To demonstrate, he lifted a rubbery leg and swung it limply.

"It's worth it," Dylan insisted, looking eagerly around for the author. "Abelard signs all these books, then I re-sell them and make a fortune. It's why I love literature."

Two well-dressed kids walked through the door of the bookshop. Ignoring the glares from those in the queue, they walked straight to the front.

"Dunstons coming through," Daine Dunston declared, smirking as she and her brother Blaine pushed past the Kirrin cousins. "Step aside."

"We get to be first, because Daddy arranged for Abelard's whole trip," Daine drawled, striking a pose at the signing table. "He knows everybody who is anybody."

Jo was unimpressed. "Does he know anyone who can make you less obnoxious?" she asked.

There was a gasp and a rustle of anticipation. A tall, lean, broad-chested and immaculately dressed teenager swept into the bookshop.

"There's no need to fear," said Abelard B. Covington grandly, "Abelard is here!" He posed, before adding in a brisk tone of voice: "Photos five pounds each."

"Mmmm," Allie sighed, looking melty around the eyes. "Why didn't anybody tell me he was a hottie?"

"So he's famous and has a lot of money," Jo growled. "What's the big deal?"

"He's famous and he has a lot of money, *that's* the big deal," Dylan explained earnestly. "*And* he has a lot of money. *And* he's famous."

Seeing his opportunity to snap a shot for his project, Max shinned up a wheeled ladder alongside a nearby bookshelf.

"Cool high-angle shot of a rich guy," he said in a pleased kind of way as he leaned precariously off the top.

Without warning, the ladder wheeled away.

"Woooaaah – ooophh . . ." Max lost his balance and plummeted to the ground. "Cool low-angle shot of the floor," he added in a muffled voice, still holding the camera to his eye.

There was a commotion at the door of the bookshop as Durwood Dunston, the red-faced and overfed father of Blaine and Daine, ran in from the street.

"Abelard! Abelard!" Mr Dunston wheezed. "You have got to help me!"

Abelard furrowed his handsome brow. "Mr Dunston," he asked with concern, "what seems to be the matter?"

"There's been a robbery!" Mr Dunston shrieked. He looked as if he was about to have a heart attack. "My Golden Chariot has been stolen! It was a gift to Julius Caesar. It's priceless! It's *gone!*"

Chapter Three

Jo started towards Mr Dunston, immediately on the alert. "What room do you keep it—"

"Fear not, Mr. Dunston," Abelard interrupted, *"I'll* soon solve this mystery."

The crowd stood agog. Abelard held out his arms to them and smiled mysteriously. "In fact," he said to his captive audience, "come along and see Abelard B. Covington solve the case as easy as A-B-C!"

"Let's beat him there," Jo said, looking irritated as Abelard breezed out of the shop followed by a swarm of admirers. *"We* should solve this mystery."

"I want to come, too," Dylan said immediately.

He held up his armful of Abelard B. Covington books. "These aren't worth anything to me if they're not signed."

Surrounded by the excitable crowd, Abelard ushered the Dunstons into his fancy car, which powered away along the street. The cousins slammed on their helmets and hopped on their bikes.

"Woaaah . . ." Dylan struggled to hang on to his stack of books as he mounted his bike and wobbled after his cousins.

The Kirrins sped along, Timmy running alongside them. Jo steered towards a nearby gate, with fields and countryside visible beyond. Just in time, Timmy leaped at the gate and pushed it open for the kids to shoot through.

Riding across a furrowed field and balancing books was not a good combination. Dylan found himself juggling Abelard B. Covington mysteries as they rumbled over the clods and lumps of earth.

"Now I know what a milk-shake feels like!" Allie said, her voice wobbling all over the place.

Taking one hand from the handlebars, Max shifted in his seat and angled his camera at Allie.

"This'll be a great photo of intense action," he announced, as the cousins jumped their bikes over a fence into a stretch of pastureland. Now Dylan was juggling, balancing *and* jumping. But he was doing better than Max, who came down right in front of the most enormous bull he'd ever seen.

"This'll be a great photo of certain doom," Max said weakly as the bull pawed the earth and snorted. He wrenched his bike sideways, causing the wheels to throw a shower of dirt into the bull's face. The beast sneezed.

"Sorry about that," Max apologised, leaping back on to his bike and pedalling like fury to catch up with his cousins.

The others had made it to the far side of the bull's field. They all sailed gracefully through the ornamental hedge that fringed the grounds of Dunston Manor, leaving neat, kid-on-bike shaped holes in the hedge as they tore on across the lawn and slid to a neatly lined-up stop on the drive. Then they hopped off their bikes and hurried into the house.

The Chariot Room was a large, grand space

hung with expensive paintings and other ancient objects – not least of which was the Dunstons' elderly butler.

"This . . ." croaked out the butler as he showed the Five into the room, "is . . . the . . ."

"Chariot Room," Allie supplied, keen to press on.

"Chariot . . ." the butler wheezed.

"Room . . ." Allie prompted.

"Room," declared the butler, as if he hadn't heard Allie. Which in all likeliness, he hadn't. "You'll . . . notice . . . the . . ."

". . . the Chariot is missing!" Dylan said, staring at the space in the centre of the room.

"Chariot . . ." the butler mumbled on, determined to finish.

"Is missing," Jo agreed. "When did you notice it was gone? Did you hear any unusual noises?"

But before the butler could answer, a more than marginally cheesed-off voice said: *"I'll* ask the questions, thank you very much."

Abelard strode into the room, followed by Mr Dunston, Blaine and Daine. The reporter Polly Lucas and Prince Hairy the chimpanzee followed close behind.

"What *is* this rabble?" Abelard asked Mr Dunston, waving at the Five.

"Hey!" Jo said indignantly.

"Just some local losers," Blaine Dunston sneered.

Dylan blew a disgusted raspberry. The others looked at him.

"He did it," Dylan said, pointing at Prince Hairy, who grinned and gave a thumbs-up.

"That chariot is made of gold-covered ebony," Mr Dunston gabbled as Abelard glanced round the room. "Only last month, *Antiques Review* had an article about it."

Abelard began to inspect the crime scene. He moved with exaggerated, overly-theatrical motions: peering through an oversized magnifying glass, listening to the walls and sniffing the air.

"Well, we shall have to find it, shan't we?" Abelard said, taking a deep investigative sniff. "I'm confident I'll solve this as easy as A-B . . . ha-chooo!!"

Abelard looked down at Timmy, who stared back at him. Abelard recoiled, waving his hands to shoo Timmy away.

Who . . . Who . . . HA-CHOO!" Abelard sneezed.

"Who let *that* in here? GET IT OUT!"

Offended, Timmy gathered his dignity and trotted out of the room.

Suddenly Abelard froze, looking like a human gun-dog scenting a pheasant. "Wait!" He sniffed the air dramatically. "I detect traces of a rare cologne, manufactured only in eastern Europe. Moldova to be precise."

"Hey," Max said, turning to his cousins. "Constantine's from Moldova! Oooph . . ."

Max groaned as Jo and Dylan both dug him in the ribs and hissed: "Ssssshhhhh!!"

"Who's from Moldova?" Abelard enquired.

Mr Dunston's eyes glinted. "Constantine Tarlev. Not wealthy. Never trusted him."

Abelard stroked his chin. "That's interesting," he said slowly. "Very interesting indeed . . ."

"Abelard is on the case!" Polly Lucas breathlessly informed her camera. "Is our local King of Crazy Golf a thief? And later, we'll be asking: Can chocolate make you lose weight? Prince Extremely Hairy investigates . . ."

"There's no way Constantine did this," Allie said, as the Kirrins gathered to discuss the strange and unwelcome direction Abelard B. Covington's investigations were taking them in. "He's our friend. He's honest. He's hard-working . . ."

". . . he's leaving town," Jo finished an hour later, as the Kirrins stood on the edge of Constantine Tarlev's crazy golf course and watched Constantine hurriedly shutter the snack bar, grab a suitcase and toss it into the back of his battered old car. Looking nervously over his shoulder, Constantine hopped behind the wheel and sped away, the engine backfiring and coughing black smoke as the fender fell off the back and clattered into a dismal, empty silence.

"Well," said Dylan, "*that* doesn't look good."

"What if we're wrong?" Allie said anxiously. "Could Constantine really be guilty?"

"And can chocolate really make you lose weight?" Max added, deep in thought. He caught the others looking at him. "I'm only asking!" he protested.

Chapter Four

An hour or two later, the Five were cutting their way through deep forest undergrowth. An abandoned railway freight truck sat lopsided in the forest clearing ahead of them, heavily draped in ivy.

Jo pushed aside the curtain of ivy and knocked on the door. The door opened and a tall, thin man with a huge moustache emerged, looking sheepishly at his visitors.

"How did you find Constantine?" Constantine asked in his heavy east European accent.

Max scratched his head. "You kind of left a trail . . ." he said, and held up part of the gear box from Constantine's car.

Constantine swivelled his head and followed the trail of nuts, bolts, carburettor wires, car doors and general bits of rust leading from his car back out of the forest.

"Constantine needs to get new car," Constantine sighed, standing back to allow the Five to enter the railway truck.

"Constantine might need to get *lawyer*," Allie added, wrinkling her nose as she stared around the Moldovan's scruffy little hideout. "Why did you run away?"

Constantine shrugged. "Where Constantine comes from, to be accused is to be convicted. When Polly Lucas and furry chimp point finger, it is time to vamoose."

Max pulled out his ever-present camera and took a photo of Constantine. Constantine winced at the flash.

"Now could you turn to the right?" Max asked, adjusting his focus. "Could be a mug shot," he explained to Jo as she looked enquiringly at him.

Constantine shuffled obediently into position as Max fired off a couple more shots.

"I don't care what that smug Abelard says," Jo declared in between flashes, "you're innocent and we're going to prove it."

Allie blew dust off an overstuffed chair in the truck and prepared to sit down. The chair collapsed into a heap.

"And maybe we could get curtains for your windows," Allie coughed, waving her hand in the dusty air. "Make it snazzy."

Constantine brightened. "While smart Kirrins clearing name," he said hopefully, "could also keeping open Constantine's snack bar? No snack bar, no money. No money, no good."

Dylan looked stricken, then sentimental. "Money," he sighed at Constantine. "You know how to get right to my heart."

"Don't worry, Constantine," said Max. He put away his camera. "We'll keep your business open. And we'll make sure justice is done."

Constantine looked relieved, then brisk. "You must sell the fish," he advised. "It's starting to smell a little off."

That night, the Five surveyed the kitchen equipment in Constantine's snack bar – a small, rectangular hut with an opening on one side that faced out towards the crazy golf course. It was safe to say that work space was limited.

"We need to know how all this works before we open up tomorrow," Jo said, frowning at the unfamiliar equipment.

Dylan ran his hand lovingly across Constantine's cash register. "Needless to say, the cash register shall be my domain," he murmured. "I love it so."

Allie opened a cupboard door. Cans, boxes and bags of cooking supplies spilled out, and a bag of flour showered down on her.

"Phff, phfff . . ." Allie coughed and blinked, beating away the white stuff from her head. "I might straighten the pantry."

The Five set to work. Nothing was as easy as it looked. Dylan attacked the cash register like a concert pianist, his fingers flying across the keys. The register retaliated, regurgitating endless receipt tape that wrapped around everything it touched.

Jo pressed the start button of an industrial-sized dishwasher, and immediately the machine started to shake and spew out foam bubbles. Max was next to try his luck. He turned a dial on the dough-mixing machine and experimented by pressing a button on the side. A stream of dough flew out over everyone's heads and clobbered Dylan. He fell on to the cash register's keyboard – the till drawer opened and closed repeatedly, pummelling Dylan as if he was the dough.

As the Five fought to regain control, soap suds started to spread across the floor. Dough was now rising uncontrollably out of the doughnut maker, expanding like a living thing that threatened to squash the Five flat. Wielding a broom, Jo

21

whacked the dough fiercely as Timmy barked encouragement. Now thoroughly overexcited, Max aimed the jam-gun at the rogue dough, but his foot slipped in the rising soap suds and his aim went awry – catching Allie smack in the face.

Amid the chaos, Timmy was the only one to hear a noise outside the snack bar. Cocking his ear to the window, he barked sharply.

Jo looked up from where she was trying to thump the dough into submission. "What is it, Timmy?" she asked.

The Five climbed over the dough, the suds, the jam and the cash receipts and fell through the snack bar door – just in time to see a dark figure in a ski mask bending over and stuffing something into the fairy-castle golf course hole.

"Hey!" Max shouted. "The golf course is closed!"

The figure looked up – then darted away.

"Well," said Jo, stating the obvious as the Five gave chase. "*That's* suspicious . . ."

Chapter Five

Jo, Max and Timmy took off after the dark figure. Swerving away from the others, Dylan and Allie headed for the fairy castle.

The figure leaped on to a merry-go-round obstacle and spun out of sight. Jo and Timmy also jumped aboard. As the merry-go-round spun clockwise, Jo and Timmy doggedly ran anti-clockwise. On the other side of the merry-go-round, the dark figure also ran anti-clockwise – so all three were on a treadmill to nowhere.

No one can run forever – particularly if they are not actually getting anywhere.

After a while, the dark figure, clearly winded,

stopped running. In moments, Jo and Timmy caught up – and crashed right into him.

"Wooahh!" grunted the figure.

"Hey!" Jo shouted as the figure jumped off and hurried towards a Toyland-themed section of the crazy golf course. The figure took no notice of her, but dashed for a huge Jack-in-the-box obstacle.

"Pop goes the weasel!" Max shouted, popping out of the box and flashing his camera.

Blinded, the figure stumbled off towards a see-saw obstacle. Allie stood waiting for him on the low end of the see-saw with her arms crossed, blocking his path. The figure jumped . . . and landed on the up-tilted end, slamming it to the ground and firing Allie into the air.

"Hoimp!" Allie cried, turning two somersaults and landing on the fairy castle itself. "And people said I'd never use my cheerleading skills in real life," she added with satisfaction, dusting herself off.

The dark figure raced away into the shadows. Max, Jo, Dylan and Timmy joined Allie at the fairy castle, looking disconsolate.

"He got away," Jo sighed.

"There's no handsome prince in this castle," said

24

Allie, climbing down. "But look what I found!"

She held out an ornate scent bottle and a picture of the Golden Chariot, torn from a magazine.

"Cologne from Moldova," Allie announced. She unstoppered the bottle and took a sniff, before rearing backwards in disgust. "Which . . . Pewww! And this picture of the Golden Chariot in the latest issue of *Antiques Review*."

Jo snatched the picture. "That's evidence of the chariot theft! That man was planting it to frame Constantine." She looked indignant. "I tell you – criminals are just . . . *bad*."

Dylan squatted down and studied the damp ground beside the fairy castle. "Look at these footprints!" he said. "Look how deep the heel marks are!"

"I'll be the only one in my class with a photo of heel prints!" Max said, firing shots at the earth before lowering his camera and adding sheepishly, "Because nobody else would take such a dumb shot."

Allie studied the heel prints. A frown of concentration crossed her face. "Definitely not normal shoes," she said, tracing the shape. "Boots,

25

men's boots, probably Cuban style, very expensive, even in a sale."

The others looked at her, dumbfounded.

"I know footwear," Allie said modestly.

Chapter Six

The Falcongate Hotel was the smartest establishment in town. And judging from the expression on the face of the desk clerk, it wasn't the kind of place where four kids and their dog were particularly welcome either.

"But you don't understand . . ." Dylan said, as the desk clerk looked down his long nose at them. "We have urgent information for Abelard! Evidence that clears his prime suspect." He held up his stack of books, adding: "And if he could sign my books, it would really help me out . . ."

"Abelard has given strict instructions not to be disturbed!" the desk clerk said fussily.

"Please leave at once."

This approach clearly wasn't working. The Five needed to rethink – and fast.

A short while later – working on the assumption that hotel desk clerks have the memory of a gnat – Max entered alone with his camera in his hand. He strode up to the desk.

"Excuse me," Max said importantly, "could you tell me . . ." His voice trailed away, as he did a double take at the desk clerk. "Hel-lo!" he murmured, leaning closer. *"You've* got the look! Have you done any modelling?"

The clerk's cheeks flushed a pleased shade of pink as Max started snapping his camera. "Hands on hips!" Max said, shimmying around the counter with his camera levelled at the clerk the whole while. "Show me love. Show me anger. You're petulant, you're petulant!"

As he moved around for different angles, Max "accidentally" knocked over a large vase of flowers and a rack of brochures. The resounding crash brought the desk clerk to his feet. Seizing on the clerk's distraction, Jo, Allie, Dylan and Timmy rapidly tiptoed through and into the kitchen.

"On second thoughts . . . pass," said Max, backing away from the clerk. And he barrelled out through the kitchen door after the others.

Looking disappointed, the desk clerk sat back down in his chair. Dylan, wearing a false moustache, came out of the kitchen, pushing a room-service trolley and buttoning up a waiter's coat which was clearly the wrong fit. Timmy's tail stuck out from beneath the trolley's tablecloth. It was wagging.

"Timmy, settle down," Jo's voice warned from underneath the tablecloth. Her hand reached out from under the snowy white linen and pulled Timmy's tail in as Dylan pushed the trolley to the lifts.

Moments later, the Five had reached Abelard's hotel room. Dylan knocked.

"Room service!" he called.

"I'm just out of the shower," came Abelard's voice from somewhere on the other side of the door. "Wait a minute!"

Then the door opened. Max slipped inside, followed by Dylan and the trolley. Abelard had disappeared again.

"Compliments of the hotel, sir," Dylan called. He nudged the underside of the trolley with one knee. "Everybody out," he added.

Jo, Allie and Timmy emerged from beneath the tablecloth. Timmy was panting with excitement and Allie was looking green.

"Ugh, Timmy," she said, "we *really* need to discuss mouthwash."

"What's the meaning of this?" A pale, flabby, short-looking young man in a towel, with straggly wet hair pasted to his scalp, was standing and glaring at the Five.

Dylan removed the lid from a silver serving tray on the trolley with a flourish. The Abelard B. Covington mysteries lay on the tray. "We need Abelard to sign these," he said, glancing around the room. "Um . . . Where's Abelard?"

"I'm Abelard!" said the man. Then he hastily backed away into the bathroom, muttering: "Oh . . . dear."

Swiftly, Abelard B. Covington reappeared, strapped into a corset that pushed his gut-flab upwards and wearing a toupée of lustrous hair.

Allie turned to Jo and made a face. "Turns out my

'hottie' is kind of . . . doughy."

"Pardon us, O Great One," Jo said, going heavy on the sarcasm, "but we have evidence in the missing chariot case."

Timmy approached Abelard, his black and tan head cocked in interest.

"Achoo!" Abelard sneezed irritably. "I'm not interested in your amateur theories! Now, out, before I summon the authorities."

He seized the hotel door and flung it open dramatically, causing his girdle to snap and twang across the room. His flab was not a pretty sight.

A few minutes later, the Five were back on the street. Timmy sat on a bench across from the hotel, his head moving from side to side like a spectator at a complicated tennis match as the four Kirrin cousins paced back and forth in front of him, crossing each other's paths as they did so.

"That tan was spray-on, and the wig was just scary," said Allie, passing Max.

"And he was so short!" Max said, passing Jo. "He must wear seriously stacked heels!"

Jo stopped dead mid-stride. "Heels high enough to make those deep marks at the golf course?" she asked.

The others stopped and looked at her.

"But that would mean that besides being a false hottie, he's trying to frame Constantine," said Allie. "Why?"

"Maybe because 'Abelard B. Criminal' committed the burglary?" Dylan suggested. "What do you think, Jo?"

They turned as the hotel doors flapped open. Abelard, now appearing as he had looked back in the bookshop, came out, glanced furtively about and then hurried away. For such a great detective, he'd made the obvious error of failing to spot the Five watching him from across the street.

"I think this could be our chance to find out," Jo said thoughtfully.

Chapter Seven

Abelard scurried down the street, looking behind him every now and again. The Five furtively peered out from behind a telephone pole: Timmy, Jo and Dylan to one side, Max and Allie to the other.

"He's going into Tyler's Nursery," said Jo as Abelard scurried into Falcongate's foremost garden centre. "He doesn't strike me as the green-fingered type . . ."

The Five detached themselves from the telephone pole and raced for Tyler's as the doors swung closed. With jungle-like stealth – only appropriate in a place full of ferns and overheating – they moved through the stacks of ladders, bags of seed and sacks of compost that stood at every turn. At last, they spotted Abelard, talking to none other than Mr Dunston. The Five made themselves comfortable behind a set of shelves, and watched the conversation as a ceiling fan whirred noisily overhead.

"Thank you for meeting me," Abelard was saying. "How much would you consider to be a worthy reward for the return of your Golden Chariot?"

Mr Dunston tried and failed to look casual. "I should say . . . five thousand pounds?"

Abelard gave a condescending laugh. "You should say *twenty* thousand. Plus your permission to write a book about my investigation."

Mr Dunston simmered with rage, but could see that he had little choice in the matter. "Oh, very well," he blustered. "Twenty thousand it is."

"Very wise," Abelard smiled. "At three o'clock this afternoon, I will reveal the location of the chariot, and name the thief who stole it."

As Abelard and Mr Dunston shook hands and Mr Dunston headed out of the nursery, Jo turned to the others. "That's in only two hours," she said. "We don't have much time."

Keeping a careful eye on Abelard, the Five crept towards the back door, edging past the shovels, hoes and other garden implements that were stacked beside the exit. Dylan was the last out. With one last glance at the toupéed detective, he shut the door – and knocked over a shovel, which fell against a ladder with an awful clattering noise.

Abelard swung round. "Who's there?" he called. "I warn you, I have black-belts in karate and ju-jitsu!"

The ladder had now started to fall. It crashed against the rotating ceiling fan, causing it to swing over a high stack of fertilizer bags. The blades sliced open the topmost bag – and a landslide of fertilizer cascaded downwards.

"Pooooph!" Abelard screeched.

"If we don't clear Constantine's name by three o'clock," said Max, peering through the window at the fertilizer-covered Abelard, "the fertilizer's really going to hit the fan!"

Back at Jo's house, in her mother George's study, the Five gathered round Dylan's laptop. Well, there were strictly only four of them taking an interest in the images of various valuable artefacts that Dylan had pulled up from the internet. Max was setting up his latest attempt at a great shot for *One Hundred Photos – Strange, Interesting or Beautiful.*

"Every one of the robberies solved by Abelard leads to him collecting a big reward," said Dylan, staring at the vases, necklaces and assorted jewellery on the screen.

"My camera's set on auto," Max said, sounding pleased as he balanced his camera on the turntable of the old Victrola gramophone. "As it spins round, it'll take brilliant, three hundred and sixty degree shots of motion and perspective."

He switched on the turntable. It immediately flung the camera into the air and through a window, where it landed in a bucket of water.

"OK," Max said after a moment. "It won't."

"So," Jo said loudly, keen to draw her cousins' attention back to the case in hand. "Abelard steals stuff, pretends to find it, then collects the reward."

"And makes even more money by writing about it in his books," said Dylan, sounding seriously impressed. "It's brilliant!"

The others frowned at him.

"But, of course, wrong," Dylan added hastily, wiping the grin off his face. "Very, very wrong."

Timmy trotted in with Max's camera in his mouth. It was dripping on the carpet.

"Thanks, Timmy," said Max gratefully.

"Timmy," Dylan said, pointing at the pile of Abelard B. Covington mysteries, "you can bury those in the garden for me. I've had enough of Abelard books."

"If we want to prove our theory," Jo continued as Timmy obediently seized Dylan's books and trotted out with them in his mouth, "we have to find that chariot before Abelard does."

"Yeah!" Allie said indignantly. "Constantine's our friend – we've got to be *totally* focused on clearing him."

Her mobile phone rang.

"Ooh," Allie said, immediately losing any vestige of focus as she snatched it up. "I hope it's the salon – maybe my new hair conditioner's in!" She hit the green button. "Hello? . . . Ohh, hi, Aunt George!"

Down in Constantine's snack bar on the crazy golf course, Jo's mother George tried to hold the phone and avoid the fountain of ice-cream raining down onto her head at the same time. "Just a quick question," she asked breathlessly, dodging a stream of raspberry ripple, "how does one turn off the ice-cream machine? Ravi can't seem to find the switch."

Ravi was underneath the soft-serve ice-cream dispenser, fiddling hopelessly with the mechanics. As happened quite often with Jo's dad, the only visible part of him was his legs.

"And it's very sticky down here," Ravi said in a muffled voice. "Oh, but I found a penny!"

"Ah," George said, nimbly side-stepping a jet of mint choc-chip, "the red switch on the back? Thank you, dear. Constantine's snack bar is in safe hands."

Hanging up the phone, George flipped the switch in triumph. Ice cream gushed out of the top of the machine like a volcano. George stared at the chaos in consternation. "Perhaps she meant the other red switch," she said, absently licking her lips. Brightening, she added: "It's tasty, though . . ."

Chapter Eight

Back at Dunston Manor, the Five crouched behind an ornamental hedge. Lurking on Dunston property was getting to be a habit. They peered over the top, Max taking in the scene through the viewfinder of his camera.

In front of the house, two security guards in dark uniforms patrolled back and forth.

Jo held a finger to her lips and mouthed: "Shhhh!" She pointed at Dylan and Allie, gesturing silently for them to go one way. Then she pointed at Max, gesturing for him to go in a different direction. Finally she pointed at Timmy and herself in continued silence, indicating that they would take a third direction.

"Right, Jo," Max said, nodding.

"We'll head that way," Allie said.

"See you later," Dylan added cheerfully, as Jo rolled her eyes in exasperation.

Moments later, Dylan and Allie were creeping along on hands and knees by the side of the Dunstons' pond. Dylan was in front of Allie, who found herself being trailed by a string of baby ducks.

"The ducks think we're their parents," Allie said, glancing over her shoulder in amusement at the fluffy yellow family.

"Go to your room," Dylan ordered the ducks. "Do your homework. They obey better than I do," he added as the ducks scattered, quacking. Then . . . "Look at this!" he gasped, suddenly alert. "A heel print! Like at the golf course."

Allie shuffled forward and examined the prints. "Abelard was here . . ." she said.

Elsewhere on the Dunston estate, Timmy moved ahead of Jo, sniffing at the path and the beds planted with colourful, exotic flowers. Finding something caught among the flowers, he grasped it

41

between his jaws and carried it to Jo.

"What have you found, Timmy?" Jo asked in excitement, holding out her hand. "Is it a clue?"

Timmy showed her the tiny object in his jaws.

That's just wheat," Jo said in disappointment. "Not really what we're looking for."

Meanwhile, Max crept round the back of the house, still looking at the world through his camera. A broad lawn backed on to Dunston Manor, bounded by a wide cobbled path. Max scanned the ground with the viewfinder, then stopped.

"Aha!" he said in triumph.

He zoomed in on a set of tyre tracks impressed into the otherwise perfectly flat lawn. Pulling back the focus, Max saw that the tracks ran from a set of side French doors to the cobbled path at the edge of the lawn. Carefully adjusting his camera's exposure level, Max pressed the shutter. Water squirted out of the lens.

Back behind the ornamental hedge, the Five gathered to swap notes on what they had found.

"The tracks were too small for a car," Max explained, still shaking his camera dry. "I bet it

42

was some kind of big cart – one that could carry the chariot."

"But the tracks stop at the cobblestones," Allie pointed out.

Jo looked out towards the woods at the bottom of the estate, chewing absently on the stalk of wheat that Timmy had found. "Where would a thief hide something as big as the chariot?" she pondered out loud, before tucking the wheat behind her ear.

"You'd need somewhere at least as big as a large shed or a garage . . ." Dylan said with a frown.

"Oi, you! Come 'ere!"

It looked as if the security guards had finally spotted them.

Jo rolled her eyes. "Yeah, right . . ." she snorted.

The Five leaped up and scattered in two different directions. Jo, Allie and Timmy raced along a path which took them into a vast green hedge maze, followed by two of the guards. Plunging straight into the cool green depths, Jo led Allie and Timmy at speed through the maze's green corridors, making turns apparently at random.

"A maze?" Allie wailed, struggling to keep up with her fleet-footed cousin and dog. "Are you crazy? We'll never get out!"

"Relax," Jo said, making a quick dog-leg left and right. "I learned my way round here when I was little!"

They shot out the other side. Deep inside the maze they heard a thump and several shouts. It sounded like the guards had crashed headlong into one another, and were now lost.

Round the back of the house, Max and Dylan ran past an open door. Max pulled Dylan inside. They barely had time to catch their breath when they were spotted.

"Here, you two!" roared Daine Dunston.

"Stop right there!" his sister Blaine squealed at the same time.

Ignoring the twins' shouts, the boys ran up a long flight of stairs with Blaine and Daine in hot pursuit. Up ahead, a pair of ornamental shields hung on the wall.

"I . . . was . . . hoping . . ." Dylan gasped for breath, "you . . . had . . . a plan . . ."

"There's a pair of plans hanging on the wall . . ." Max panted, pointing at the shields. He stopped, grabbed a shield down from the wall and placed it

44

on the banister. Then in one smooth move, he
jumped on to the shield and slid downwards.
Copying his cousin, Dylan grabbed the second
shield, placed it on the banister and jumped aboard
as well.

"Yeah!" Max screamed.

"Whoooaaah!" Dylan yelled as they surfed
expertly down the stairwell.

Shooting off the end of the banister, they surfed

on across the polished hall floor, heading for the huge front door.

"Waaaaaaaaahhhhhhhhh!" Max and Dylan shrieked, bursting through the door, bumping down the front steps, shooting across the lawn, and catching the slope that led down to the pond – into which they disappeared with an almighty splash.

After a moment, they came spluttering to the surface.

"My camera is never going to dry out," Max croaked. He did a double take into the pond's depths. "Ooh – a carp!"

Chapter Nine

A crowd of interested onlookers had gathered on the Dunstons' drive. Among them were Polly Lucas, Prince Hairy, Blaine, Daine and a scowling Mr Dunston. Their heads turned as one at the roar of an engine approaching up the drive. Abelard's car was driving towards them at speed.

The car screeched to a halt, sending a shower of grit over the crowd. "There's no need to fear," Abelard declared, emerging from the car and striking a pose, "Abelard is here!"

There was a smattering of applause.

"I intend to reveal the location of the chariot," Abelard announced. "My usual study of the facts has again succeeded in piercing the veil of mystery . . ."

Timmy wove through the legs of the transfixed crowd as Abelard warmed to his theme. He trotted over to the low wall and hopped over to find Max and Dylan hiding in uncomfortable, crouched, damp positions. Dylan plucked a note from under Timmy's collar and unfolded it.

"Follow Timmy," Dylan read.

Once he was sure Dylan and Max had read and understood their instructions, Timmy headed away. Bent double, Max and Dylan obediently followed.

The pair of security guards had found their way out of the maze. Nursing bruised heads, they were now stalking between the assortment of ancient and modern statues dotted about the Dunstons' lawn. One of the guards peered at a hand-held radar tracker, before shaking his head and motioning for his partner to follow him to a different section of the grounds.

Jo poked her head out from behind one of the sculptures. "Come out, come out wherever you are!" she called softly.

The rest of the Five emerged from behind their different statues, shaking their limbs out of the statue poses they had been forced to adopt.

"Abelard's still yacking on about how he solved the crime," Dylan told the others. "We've got maybe five minutes before he 'finds' the chariot!"

Allie saw the wheat stalk still stuck behind Jo's ear. "Hey, Jo," she said, "I didn't notice before. But the little 'Nature Girl' vibe you've got going kinda works . . ."

Jo looked puzzled, then removed the stalk of wheat from her ear. "It's not a 'Nature Girl' vibe. It's wheat – Timmy found it in the flower beds." She considered the wheat, frowning. "There's an old granary at the bottom of the property," she said at last.

"Is it as big as a large shed or a garage?" said Dylan pointedly.

Leaving Abelard declaiming to his audience, the Five sneaked away from the ornamental hedge and made their way to the granary. It was large and tucked away – the perfect hiding place for a stolen artefact as large as the chariot?

Timmy barked as the Five swept the ground

49

around the granary for clues. Dylan bent down to examine Timmy's discovery.

"Timmy's found more of Abelard's heel-prints," Dylan announced, grinning at the others. "He was here!"

"This padlock's brand new," Max said, tugging at the bright new lock on the granary's heavy oak doors. "Abelard could've hidden the chariot in here, and the wheat you found could've hitched a ride on his boot."

Jo studied the granary with a frown, her eyes resting at last on a small window high up near the roof. "The only way in is up there," she said, pointing.

The Five stared up. The wall to the window looked steep and pretty much unclimbable.

"If only we had a ladder or—" Dylan began.

"Or the leader of the three-time Tri-State Cheerleading Champions?" Allie put in coyly.

Before long, the four cousins had made a human pyramid for Allie to climb up. Max and Dylan held firm at the base, and Jo stood on their shoulders.

"This routine won us our third title . . ." Allie reminisced as she climbed up her cousins. "Of course, we had cute outfits." She reached the top of the pyramid and steadied herself. *"It doesn't matter if it's hard, We will stop that Abelard!"* Allie cried, cheerleader-style. *"Go, Kirrins!"* And she squeezed herself through the window and out of sight.

"Oooph," Jo grunted as she jumped off Max and Dylan's shoulders.

"The chariot's in here!" Allie squealed from inside the granary. "Eeew! So's a huge, gross rat! Get away! Shoo!"

CLANG!

To Jo, Max and Dylan's astonishment, a delivery door suddenly opened in the granary wall.

"Well done, Allie!" Jo cheered, recovering first. "But how—"

Allie appeared in the door in the wall and gestured to a metal lever which was sticking out into the opening. "I grabbed that bar to chase away the rat," she said, holding the bar to illustrate. "It's the lever that opens the loading door." She pulled the lever and the door shut. "See?" she said, pleased. "Open, close, open, close, open . . ."

The cousins and Timmy ducked through the opening – just as Abelard appeared, leading his group toward the granary.

"Uh-oh," said Allie, quickly flipping the lever again. "Close!"

The opening swung shut just as Abelard laid his hand on the granary's great oak door. ". . . and so you see, ladies and gentlemen," he said, producing a pair of bolt-cutters and cutting through the padlock, "once again, I have solved the mystery as easy as . . ."

He swung the door open, revealing the Five standing in the glittering Golden Chariot inside the granary.

"A-B-C," Jo said helpfully as Abelard looked stunned. "Abelard Burgled the Chariot."

Chapter Ten

Abelard opened and closed his mouth like a particularly stupid goldfish as he stared at the Five. "That's ridiculous!" he stuttered, recovering. "Absurd! Preposterous!"

"Then why are your footprints all round here and up by the house?" Allie challenged.

Max folded his arms and fixed his eyes on the sweating detective. "And why would you try to plant evidence to frame Constantine?"

The onlookers and media crowded in on Abelard like a wave.

"Abelard," said Polly Lucas, thrusting her microphone under Abelard's nose, "what are they talking about?"

"Who knows?!" Abelard spluttered. "I am Abelard, the master detective! I – I . . ."

"We've got the cologne bottle . . . and the *Antiques Review* picture," said Dylan. "You saw the article and decided the chariot would be 'Abelard's next case', right?"

"I've even got a shot of you at the golf course!" said Max, holding up his camera.

Abelard grabbed Max's camera, pushed the rest of the Five off the chariot and leaped aboard. His weight caused the chariot to roll off the wheeled dolly it was sitting on, plunge out of the granary and head downhill towards an old cemetery.

The Five grabbed the dolly, pushing it after Abelard like a toboggan team starting down an ice chute.

"After him!" Max yelled, leaping aboard. "He's got my photo assignment!"

The dolly took off down the hill after the chariot, leaving the gasping spectators behind. Up ahead, Abelard clung to the chariot as it blasted though the old wooden gate of the cemetery and bounced over the uneven ground, cannoning off the old, sunken gravestones.

"Wooaah – ohhh – wayyyyyy," Abelard squealed, almost falling out of the chariot as he was knocked about.

The Five leaned this way and that as a team, shifting their weight to steer the dolly between the gravestones.

"LEFT!" Jo roared. "RIGHT! MIDDLE! STEADY!"

The chariot smashed through a rickety fence on the far side of the cemetery and straight into the vegetable garden on the other side. A scarecrow wrapped Abelard in an affectionate hug, but Abelard managed to pry it off and toss it back towards the Kirrins.

"Oooff," Dylan spluttered as the scarecrow caught him full-on. "Welcome aboard."

The Five were gaining on Abelard. The dolly drew up alongside the chariot, and they shifted their weight so the dolly veered into the chariot, altering its course.

"I think he's heading in the right direction now," Jo gasped as the chariot bounced on down the hill towards a copse of trees.

"Mind if I borrow your collarbone?" Dylan asked

the scarecrow politely, pulling the broomstick handle that constituted the scarecrow's shoulders and handing it to Max.

Max thrust the broomstick into the spokes of the chariot wheel. The chariot instantly stopped, catapulting Abelard through the air.

"WAAAAAAAAAAAAAHHHHHHHHHH!!!!" Abelard wailed, cartwheeling into the trees — and smashing straight into the side of Constantine's railway truck hideout. He slid down its ivy-covered side and landed in a senseless heap with his toupée askew. Last of all, his girdle burst, revealing Abelard's gut to a group of startled woodland animals and Constantine himself, who had emerged from the truck with toothpaste around his mouth and a startled expression.

The Five zoomed in to the forest clearing, still aboard their dolly.

"I didn't know you got a shot of him at the golf course," Dylan said to Max as they stared at the unconscious villain on the ground.

"I didn't!" Max said. "I was bluffing . . . But it worked, right?" He seized his camera from Abelard and started clicking away.

"That'll make a good photo for the cover of his next book," Jo observed. *"Abelard And The Really Long Prison Sentence."*

"That I would want to get signed," Dylan agreed.

In the crazy golf course snack bar later that day, the Five were gathered around Constantine. Constantine looked delighted to be home, and kept stroking his cash register.

"Constantine is indebted to Kirrins for sparing him eternity in prison," he smiled warmly, patting the doughnut-making machine. "So, doughnuts for Kirrins!"

"Wow," said Dylan in delight. "Free doughnuts!"

"Not free," Constantine said. "Ten per cent off. Constantine still businessman. But – *freshly made* doughnuts . . ."

"Allow me," said Max. He flexed his fingers and pressed the start button on the doughnut-maker. It instantly started spewing out dough – along with the ice-cream maker spraying soft-serve ice-cream, the dishwasher overflowing with suds and the cash register drawer leaping open and shut.

"I might have hit the wrong button . . ." said Max, looking perplexed.

Constantine laughed good-naturedly as Timmy started lapping up the ice cream. "Kirrins will clean up," he said. And he handed Dylan a mop, put his hat on and left them to it.

Epilogue

Out in the woods the following day, it was Dylan's turn with the videocamera.

"Sticky Situation Number Thirty-Five," he said, angling the camera at a group of trees. "You Have To Hide."

Wearing green clothes, Max stepped out from behind a tree next to some shrubs. "Sometimes you have a good hiding place, but sometimes you have to make one," he informed Dylan's camera. "Undergrowth can make good camouflage, and you can blend into the surroundings."

As he picked up branches and grass and rubbed mud on his face, arms and clothes, Max glanced around. "In fact," he said with a frown, "Jo has camouflaged herself so well, no one can find her."

Timmy trotted up to one of the shrubs and sniffed it. His tail wagged, and the shrub started getting a thorough licking.

"Timmy," said the shrub, "stop it!"

"No one except Timmy," Max added.

"Stop!" wailed the Jo-shrub, leaping on to a pair of green legs and running away as Timmy's tongue pushed in among its branches. "I'm ticklish!"

pretty, long-haired young woman in an elegant medieval dress was smiling on his arm.

"Home to the noble King Oliver," Jo continued, "the fair Princess Petula . . ."

"And the Dark Prince Roland!" Max added.

They all stared at the young man with dark hair, wearing a suit of armour with a wooden sword at his side, who was glowering at King Oliver as he raised a golden goblet in salute.

Timmy the dog took a long, appreciative sniff at Prince Roland.

"It sounds so fun," Allie said, peering over her cousins' shoulders as they all stared at the glossy holiday brochure in Jo's hands. "I can't wait to go. Let's see, I'll need my scrunchies, my travel make-up case—"

"We have to live just like they did in the Middle Ages," tomboy Jo reminded her looks-obsessed cousin with a grin. "No make-up."

"Oh," Allie said. She pulled a face. "I'm not going."

Max looked at Allie from beneath his shaggy blond fringe. The fringe made him look like a dog that was after a treat. "But that's the fun of it!" he said. "It's all old-school. Being chivalrous, eating turkey legs, wiping your hands off on the dog . . ."

Timmy withdrew his nose from the brochure and retreated to a safe distance.

"Probably no computers," Dylan said dismissively. Computers were Dylan's world. "No wonder they called it the Dark Ages."

Allie was looking interested again. "But they did have princesses, right?" she checked. Princesses were big in California. "Ooh, I can be a princess! OK, I'll go – it'll be fun."

"Fun?!" Dylan snorted, looking unimpressed. "Try dull. Nothing exciting ever happened in the Middle Ages."

Back on Avalon Island, King Oliver, Princess Petula and Prince Roland were drinking a toast from their goblets. Suddenly, Prince Roland dropped his goblet and staggered forward. His face turned pale. He grabbed his throat, gurgled frantically and toppled to the floor. Stone dead . . .

Read the adventures of George and the
original Famous Five in

THE
FAMOUS FIVE'S
SURVIVAL GUIDE

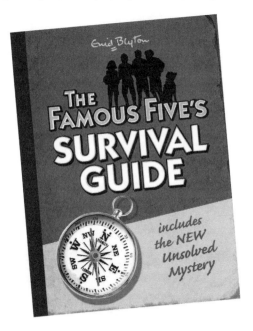

Packed with useful information on surviving outdoors and solving mysteries, here is the one mystery that the Famous Five never managed to solve. See if you can follow the trail to discover the location of the priceless Royal Dragon of Siam.

The perfect book for all fans of mystery, adventure and the Famous Five!

ISBN 9780340970836